For Tom & Penny Worrell
— G. S.

To my faithful assistant, Molly
— D. Z.

Text copyright © 2005 by George Shannon

Illustrations copyright © 2005 by Deborah Zemke

CIP Data is available

Published in the United States in 2005 by Handprint Books

413 Sixth Avenue

Brooklyn, New York 11215

www.handprintbooks.com

First Edition

Printed in China

ISBN: 1-59354-118-X trade

ISBN: 1-59354-128-7 library

2 4 6 8 10 9 7 5 3 1

The Secret Chicken Club

By **George Shannon**

Illustrations by **Deborah Zemke**

Handprint Books ✋ Brooklyn, New York

Knock, Knock

EACH day at Wise Acres was a day to celebrate. The sun always came up. There was plenty of food. And lightning bugs never thundered at night.

Debbie loved to dance. Some days she practiced ballet. Other days, she tapped. She devoted weekends to the Highland fling.

One day as she danced her cow-fairy dance, she heard Blanche whisper, "Pssst. Doug! The Secret Chicken Club will meet tonight. Pass it on."

Debbie's heart jumped. She decided to start a Secret Cow Club. Then her shoulders drooped. She was the only cow on the farm. And she couldn't have a Secret Cow Club with only one cow.

Debbie danced toward Blanche.

"Please," asked Debbie, "may I join your club?"

"Heavens, no!" said Blanche. "It's just for chickens."

Debbie flapped her arms. "But I could *act* like one."

"Maybe," said Blanche. "As club president I can give you a test. You have to cluck, lay an egg, and eat ten worms."

For five straight days, Debbie tried to cluck and
lay an egg. For five straight nights, she tried to eat
worms. She almost clucked, but she gagged every time
she held a worm near her lips. Worst of all, she kept
falling off the nest without laying so much as one
scrambled egg.

On the sixth day, Vannah found Debbie stuck halfway through the door of the chicken coop.

"I'll never get to be in a secret club," sobbed Debbie as the chickens pulled her out. "And *your* secret club is the very best."

Blanche and Doug's eyes filled with tears at the thought of being excluded from the club.

"All right," said Blanche. "If you pass the next test you may join our Secret Chicken Club."

"Knock, knock," said Blanche.

Debbie grinned. "Who's there?"

"Repeat."

"Repeat who?"

"Who, who, who," said all the chickens. "Who, who, who."

Debbie laughed so hard, milk came out of her nose.

"Welcome to the club!" said Blanche. "Only Secret Club members like our favorite joke."

Blanche

Bob and Ray gave Debbie an old tin funnel to wear as a beak. Doug taught her the secret password.

"Oh!" said Debbie.

"*Shsssssssh,*" said Doug. "That's it. But never say the password when others might hear."

Then they sang the club song with a mouthful of corn to make sure no one could understand the secret words.

Clargh auh augh afh
Auck clugh uh augh
Acgh uck auh auckkkkkkkkkkkk!

Debbie spun with joy. "Let's do the club dance."

"The club *what*?" said Doug.

Blanche gasped. "I never thought about a dance."

"Then follow me," Debbie stepped to the front.

"I'm going to teach you the Secret Chicken Coop!"

"Make your feet the foundation. Make your stomach the walls. Arms shape the roof. Now, pretend you're full of straw. Feel it in your hips as you cluck with luck. We're doing the coop with a *boop-boop-dee-doop*!"

"*Boop-boop-dee-doop-boop-dee-boop-boop-dee-COOP!*"

Brain Food

DOUG crowed up the sun and headed for the road.

"How long will you be gone?" asked Roy.

"I suspect the whole time," said Doug. "But my answer could change once I get the brain food."

"Brain food?"

"A vitamin soup that makes a chicken's noodle even smarter than before," Doug pointed to his head. "A noodle like mine can never be too sharp!"

"Can you get me some?" asked Roy. "I wouldn't mind a little brain boost myself."

"Sorry," Doug explained. "It's just for those of us who know the password to the Secret Chicken Club."

Roy sighed. "Oh."

"My mistake!" said Doug. "I apologize. I didn't know *you'd* become a member of the Secret Chicken Club. I'll get you a can of your very own."

Roy shook his head as Doug wandered on his way. "What? Secret chickens with clubs?"

"Where are you going?" called Vern.

"Into town," Doug said with a grin. "To get a vitamin soup that makes a chicken's noodle even smarter than before."

"Can you get me some?" Vern tapped his head. "I wouldn't mind a boost in the brain myself."

"Sorry," Doug explained. "It's a soup just for those of us who know the password to the Secret Chicken Club."

Vern sighed, "Oh."

"My mistake!" said Doug. "I didn't know *you'd* become a member of the Secret Chicken Club. I'll get you a can of your very own."

Vern blinked and scratched his head as Doug continued down the road.

As Doug passed the pond, Pearl shook her tambourine.

"Where are you going?" she called.

"Into town," said Doug, "for a vitamin soup I just heard about. It makes a chicken even smarter than before."

"Even smarter?" said Ted. "Will you get us some?"

"Sorry," said Doug. "It's just for those of us who know the password to the Secret Chicken Club."

"Says who?" demanded Pearl.

Doug laughed. "The *can*, that's who. Use your noodle and think. If this brain food was meant for everyone, it wouldn't be called Chicken Noodle Soup."

"But you can't!" Pearl's eyes popped wide.

"Sure I can," said Doug. "I'm getting Chicken Noodle Soup for every chicken's noodle in the club."

Ted clutched his heart. Pearl whispered to Doug.

"Don't be silly." Doug laughed. "Debbie eats tapioca to help her tap-dance."

"Of course it helps," said Pearl. "But soup's a different thing. Use your noodle and think. Tomato soup is made with tomatoes. Bean soup is made with beans. Soups are named for what goes inside."

Doug's legs began to shake. "You mean—"

Pearl and Ted nodded. "Chicken Noodle Soup has chicken noodles—chicken brains—inside."

Doug fell flat on the ground, beak and toes to the sun. "I could have lost my mind," he moaned. "How do you keep your noodle so sharp?"

"Simple." Pearl smiled. "I use it so rarely, it never has a chance to get worn out!"

Thief!

EVERYWHERE Debbie looked, the meadow was a blooming, sweet bouquet.

"Divine!" she announced. "Perfect for rehearsing my recital for the Secret Chicken Club.

Debbie untied her tin beak and laid it down in
her shadow on the ground. "Wouldn't want this
to get hot in the sun," she said.

"Dance like the breeze," she sang to herself
and began to skip. "Dance like the wind!"

She turned with a leap. She twirled and
hopped. Then she criss cross-stepped, spun
around, and bowed.

Debbie practiced over and over again.

"*Ta-dah!*" Debbie gasped for breath. "This recital will be my best."

She turned to get her beak, but it wasn't in her shadow. It wasn't anywhere! Debbie needed help from Stella, ace detective, and she needed it now.

"Stella!" cried Debbie as she ran to the barn. "Help, Stella, help! Someone stole my beak. I left it in my shadow, and now it's gone!"

"AHA!" Stella quickly took charge and glared at Bob and Ray. "Where were *you* this afternoon?"

"In the barn," said Bob.

"With *you*," said Ray.

Stella turned to Janet. "Where were *you* this afternoon?"

"In the barn with *you*."

Every answer was the same till it was Debbie's turn.

"In the meadow," Debbie said with a sniff, "rehearsing my recital for the Secret Chicken Club."

"I see." Stella spoke in her lowest voice. "Did anyone see you?"

Debbie squeaked, "No."

"AHA!" cried Stella. "No witnesses. And you were the last one to see the beak. *You're* the thief! Everyone follow me to the scene of the crime."

Stella led them east to the meadow as the sun began to set.

"My beak?" Debbie ran as her shadow led the way. "It's here! It was in my shadow where I left it all along."

"AHA!" Stella bowed. "The perfect mystery. No clues. No witnesses. And now, no crime! Another case closed."

"Oh!" gasped everyone.

Debbie blinked with surprise. "When did *all* of *you* learn the password to the Secret Chicken Club?"

"What club?" grumbled Janet.

"I get it." Debbie winked. "You've got to keep it a secret when you're in a secret club."

Now that the Secret Chicken Club included everyone, Debbie danced her recital right there and then while the whole farm sang the Secret Chicken Club song.

Clargh auh augh afh
Auck clugh uh augh
Acgh uck auh auckkkkkkkkkkkk!

With so much in common, life at Wise Acres
wandered on with ease. Dancing, laughter, songs,
and food. And the shared delight that they all had
a birthday in the very same year.